Everyone Makes a Difference!

Duane Whitely

Proverbs 3:5 & 6

# GILLIGAN,
# the Donkey
## that Got a
# Second Chance

ISBN 979-8-88616-655-2 (paperback)
ISBN 979-8-88751-414-7 (hardcover)
ISBN 979-8-88616-656-9 (digital)

Christian Faith Publishing
832 Park Avenue
Meadville, PA 16335
www.christianfaithpublishing.com

Printed in the United States of America

# GILLIGAN, the Donkey
## that Got a
# Second Chance

written by
## Duane Whitely

illustrated by
## Natia Gogiashvili

On a farm to the north,
across the state line;
a donkey had lived there
for quite a long time.

The farm had some chickens,
and an old dog that growls;
and a donkey called Gilligan,
in a field with some cows.

He was a small little guy,
dark brown and some tan;
He liked carrots and apples,
he'd take right out of your hand.

Now donkeys are known,
for protection of herds;
but the cows HE was with,
thought that he was absurd.

See, they were bigger than him,
and they felt quite secure;
they said cows of THEIR size,
didn't need him for sure.

So he stayed to himself,
and felt invisible most days;
with his eyes to the ground,
he never took time to play.

Now the farmer had no use,
for a donkey so small;
so he posted an ad,
and then hoped for a call.

Then one day, Gilligan was grazing,

and of course, all alone.

When a man and a lady,

drove up on their own.

The farmer came out,
and they talked for a while;
then the man looked at Gilligan,
and he had a big smile.

"He's just what we want,"
the lady smiled and agreed;
so she came through the gate,
with a halter and a lead.

Gilligan lifted his chin,
like a crook to be cuffed;
then she slipped on the halter,
and they walked toward the truck.

The man backed up their trailer,
and swung open the door;
Gilligan walked right straight in,
as he STOMPED on the floor.

Now he never looked back,
'cause there was nothing to see;
he just looked straight ahead,
and thought what his new life would be.

Back there he was laughed at,
and made fun of a lot;
he didn't know now,
but a second chance he just got.

After a while in the trailer,
and a long bumpy ride;
the truck came to a stop;
he wondered what was outside.

Gilligan tried to peek out,
but the sides were too high;
he had a knot in his stomach;
then the door opened wide!

He slowly peeked out,
then he waited awhile;
he saw the man and the lady,
and they both had a smile.

He looked all around,
and thought why he was here.
Was he having a dream?
Was all this for real?

He had a strange feeling,
and wondered, would he fit in?
he looked up at the man,
and he saw that big grin!

Gilligan didn't know why,
but now he felt real good;
'cause the animals here,
seemed all in a good mood.

All the people were friendly,
he had grain and fresh hay,
little kids waved their hands;
like they wanted to play.

So as days turned to weeks,
and weeks into months;
he had found a new home,
and made friends he could trust.

There was a big flock of sheep,
little lambs having fun;
a coop full of chickens,
a lot of work to be done.

If a fox or a coyote,
would happen around;
he would let out a warning,
a most bone-curdling sound.

First he'd bray, then he'd squeal,
and if that didn't help;
he'd clear out his throat,
and let out a big *yelp*!

Then he'd stomp on the ground,
and run up and down;
and make all of the animals,
know that danger's around.

That's all that he wanted,
to be useful and liked;
he had got "a second chance,"
he knew things would be all right.

When he gets up each morning,
he'll look all around;
like a guard on a tower,
a new sheriff's in town.

So if you're a fox or a coyote,
or a weasel or hawk;
you better just move along,
better watch where you walk.

'Cause if you're looking for dinner,
you'll find nothing here;
but a donkey with attitude,
so you better steer clear.

So if people would look at people,
and not judge them at a glance;
then people who really need it,
Might get that second chance!

Then at night, when it's quiet,
Gilligan twitches his ear;
and he closes "one" eye,
and a small grin will appear.

Then just before he drifts off,
he'll think back for a while;
of the second chance that he got,
and that man's great big smile.

# About the Author

Duane was born and raised in Harford County, Maryland, and has enjoyed volunteering at the Restoration Farm. At the farm, an all-volunteer staff care for many different farm animals and offer AG Education, outdoor activities, and Christian-based community service programs.

CPSIA information can be obtained
at www.ICGtesting.com
Printed in the USA
JSHW020608031222
33874JS00002BH/11